For Ella, with love – *AM*

For Missy – *JC*

First published in Great Britain in 2003 by Bloomsbury Publishing Plc
38 Soho Square, London, W1D 3HB

A CIP catalogue record of this book is available from the British Library
ISBN 0 7475 5921 X

Designed by Sarah Hodder

Printed in Hong Kong/China

1 3 5 7 9 10 8 6 4 2

Blue Rabbit

by Angela McAllister

illustrated by Jason Cockcroft

BLOOMSBURY
CHILDREN'S
BOOKS

Blue Rabbit slept in a very big bed with a very big pillow.
He couldn't reach the bottom with his toes. He couldn't
reach the top with the tips of his ears.
But Blue Rabbit didn't feel lost in the very big bed
because every night he had his Boy to cuddle.

Boy always understood if Blue Rabbit was worried or sad.

Boy always helped if Blue Rabbit was puzzled or stuck.

Boy was soft and warm and stuffed with love, and each night they fell asleep together in the very big bed.

But one evening Blue Rabbit couldn't find his Boy.
"Where did you see him last?" asked the toys.
Blue Rabbit couldn't remember. "He was here
this morning and now he's lost."

The toys agreed to help. They hunted in all the usual places. Then they hunted in unusual places. But Boy was nowhere to be found.

The house grew dark and the toys grew sleepy.
"Don't worry," they said, "he'll turn up tomorrow."

For the first time Blue Rabbit's big bed felt cold and lonely.
He climbed in and pulled the covers up to his chin. "I can't go to sleep without my Boy," he said in a small voice.

Creepy shadows darted across the ceiling. Night noises teased and tricked. Blue Rabbit thought he heard something rustle under the bed. He didn't feel brave without his Boy, but he had to look …

Slowly, holding on to the very big pillow, he tried to peer under the bed. Further and further he stretched until …

... out he fell with a bump!

A mouse scampered up. "Have you seen my Boy?" asked Blue Rabbit.
But the mouse just shook her head and ran away.

Blue Rabbit climbed back into bed. He told himself a story but he couldn't get to sleep without his Boy. So he sat up all night long, closing first one eye and then the other until morning.

The next day Boy was still lost. Maybe he was left in the garden. Blue Rabbit waited by the back door but it never opened.

Once again the toys hunted up and down, inside
and behind, on top and underneath. Blue Rabbit sat
on the bottom stair and watched the front door.

Suddenly Monkey called out, "I've found him, he's here."
At last! Blue Rabbit jumped up and ran. Monkey was
doing somersaults on the carpet.

He pointed up to the mantelpiece.

Blue Rabbit's heart sank.

"Oh dear," said Old Brown Dog.

"It's only a photograph."

For the rest of the day Blue Rabbit sat beside the photograph.
When it grew so dark that he could no longer see his Boy,
Blue Rabbit whispered, "I will never forget you, never,"
and trudged sadly up to bed.

That night Old Brown Dog shuffled into Blue Rabbit's room.
"I shall keep you company," he said, and climbed up beside his friend.

Old Brown Dog was kind and soft and warm, but he wasn't Boy.
Blue Rabbit felt empty inside as if all his stuffing had been pulled out.

Day after day Blue Rabbit hunted for his lost Boy until there was nowhere left to look. So he just sat sadly on the mantelpiece. Although he didn't play with the toys any more they all squeezed into the very big bed at night to keep him company.

As more days passed Blue Rabbit's whiskers drooped and his eyes lost their sparkle. He didn't even bother to get out of bed. With his eyes shut he could smell Boy, as if he were somewhere near.

"You must forget him," said Old Brown Dog.
"Boy has gone to the place where all lost things go."
"Where ears go," said the one-eared bear,
"and drum sticks and pieces of jigsaw puzzle."

"No," said Blue Rabbit. "I'll never forget." And he burrowed under the covers and began to cry. He cried and cried and cried. He cried so hard that he didn't hear the key in the front door. He cried so loudly that he didn't hear running footsteps on the stairs. He shut his eyes so tight that he didn't see the covers pulled back until … there was Boy, home from his holiday!

Once more Blue Rabbit's whiskers bristled and his eyes sparkled. Could it really be true? Boy was different somehow … Boy had turned a rusty brown colour and his clothes had all shrunk. "I suppose he must have been left out in the garden, in the rain," thought Blue Rabbit.

But when they hugged each other tight,
Blue Rabbit knew his Boy hadn't really
changed at all. For he was still soft and
warm and stuffed with love.